LAUREL LA

The Other Man

A novella by Laurel Landon

2/14/2017

This book contains erotic scenes and is for readers over 18 years of age.

Copyright © 2014 by Laurel Landon

All rights reserved.

No part of this book may be reproduced or transmitted in any form or by any means, electronic or mechanical, including photocopying, recording, or by information storage and retrieval system without the written permission of the author, except for the use of brief quotations in a book review.

This book is a work of fiction. Any resemblance to actual persons, living or dead, events, or locations is purely coincidental. All rights reserved. Except as permitted, under the U.S. Copyright Act of 1976, no part of this publication may be reproduced, distributed, or transmitted in any form or by any means, or stored in a database or retrieval system, without the prior express, written consent of the author.

Violation of copyright, by domestic or foreign entities, is punishable by law, which may include imprisonment, a fine, or both.

This book is intended for mature audiences only.

Contents

Acknowledgements 4
Dedication 5
Prologue 7
Chapter 1 17
Chapter 2 25
Chapter 3 39
Chapter 4 47
Epilogue 67
Epilogue-Preston's POV 75
Epilogue - Ethan's POV 92
About the Author 95
Sneak Peek! (From "Dark Ride") 97

Acknowledgements

To all of my readers of Hello Dolly, Sherry Darling, Dark Ride and Making the Team who begged for more steam and taboo! You got it!!

Dedication

This book is dedicated to all women out there who can identify with Rian. Don't ever settle, and if you do, don't ever feel like you have!

Prologue

My name is Rian and I'm pretty sure that you're not going to like me. In fact, I'd bet the rent on it, except that well . . . I don't *pay* rent, you see. Someone else does that for me.

His name is Preston Barringer II.

Does that name ring a bell?

If you're from the East Coast it might, provided you shop for men's couture. Barringer's is the most exclusive carrier of men's fine clothing, with stores in New York City, Philadelphia, Boston, Atlanta New Orleans and Miami.

Preston is the older of two sons, thus the Roman numeral two after his name. Preston Barringer, the first, is now retired and living the good life in Miami with his wife and his millions.

With me so far?

Good.

Now, let's get to the part where you're going to judge me. And you very well might have legitimate reasons to do so.

Preston is forty-four years old, rich, handsome and totally . . . married. He has three children, lives in the affluent Chestnut Hill section of Boston, and has an exquisite wife from another prominent New England family.

They attend every social event of the season, Christmas being an especially busy time of the year for those. Their children attend the very best private schools, where they receive academic accolades every semester. For all intents and purposes, the Barringer family is picture perfect.

With one exception--one dark, dirty little secret that is hidden from the public eye.

Me.

Rian Elizabeth Roberts, age thirty-one, former model and present mistress, lover, whore--whatever you wish to label me to Preston Barringer II.

So, there it is for you to digest with the usual female emotions ranging from disgust to ambivalence, depending upon your own personal life experiences or internal judgments with this sort of thing.

Maybe you've even been in my shoes. (Hope they're Gucci or Jimmy Choo's because that's what Preston keeps me in these days.) Or maybe you've been the poor, unsuspecting wife, in which case you probably don't want to read any further. In your opinion, I'm nothing short of a home wrecking, artist of seduction, and trashy tramp, right?

Wrong.

That's *not* how it happened, trust me, and also believe me when I say that it has very little to do with you. I mean, that's *exactly* what he's going to say to you if you ever discover me. 'It has nothing to do with you, or how I feel about you.'

And guess what?

That *is* the truth. Women don't see it that way, of course. They presume it is a reflection in some way of their failure to please him at home, in bed, or perhaps their physical and/or sexual attractiveness has diminished over the years.

All totally false.

The truth is that men cheat because they *can*. So, hate me if you must, but just remember, if it's not me, it *will* be someone else. And that someone else may not be as introspective, benevolent and altruistic as me.

Oh, I'm not trying to paint myself as some adult girl scout here; not at all. But the truth is that I don't want to wreck Preston's marriage; I don't want to replace Emily (his wife). I am perfectly happy and content with his attention and generosity--for the most part that is.

At least I was until recently.

I've been feeling trapped and restless lately. I've developed a curiosity of how life might be without the bonds that Preston has placed on me. Someone I haven't met has planted seeds of doubt in my mind, or maybe they've always been there waiting for me to acknowledge them.

Let's face it; holidays are a bummer for a lot of reasons. But each year for the past three, Preston sends me on a trip for most of December and through the first week of January. He allows me to choose where I want to go. I think it eases his conscience a bit knowing that I'm not holed up and alone in my apartment.

Yes, I said *conscience*. Don't believe that old saying, "A dick has no conscience," because it's just not true.

Let me back up for a second. Preston and I met a little over three years ago while I was doing a photo shoot for GQ magazine. The ad showed me dressed in a tight little black dress, wearing fuck-me pumps, and pulling a gorgeous male model behind me by the necktie he was wearing. Of course, his business suit was one of Barringer's finest. Preston personally oversees all of the marketing and advertising copy. He's OCD about it actually.

So when he invited me out for a drink after the shoot, I gladly accepted. Drinks then turned into dinner, and eventually . . . breakfast. I can honestly say I did not know that he was married at that time. I learned shortly afterward when he expressed a desire to see me again, even providing me with his private cell number and instructions to leave a message because he never answers it.

I guess maybe I was a bit floored at the time, but of course I tried my best not to show it. I keep my past hidden from everyone, because actually, it's quite uninspired.

I don't come from wealth or privilege. I never knew my father, though my mother assured me that I had one out there . . . somewhere. She couldn't quite remember his name though, but apparently he was special to her, because he was the only one of her regulars that she allowed to disregard the condom code. She said that he paid her $50 more to ride her bareback.

Once I was well underway, she had to give up her career as a pro. She never held that against me, in fact, all things considered, my mother did the best that she could having a child at nineteen-- circumstances being what they were back then.

So, anyway, having been raised by the daughter of a Baptist minister turned whore, and moving sometimes three or four times a year to different trailer parks, kind of made me grow up fast--and wiser for it. . . I think.

I knew that it wouldn't take much to have a better life than Mom, and she always told me that my beauty would see to that; I made sure that it did.

My mother passed away shortly after I turned nineteen. The coroner ruled her death as an accidental overdose, but I knew better. It was suicide, pure and simple. She'd always told me that she was holding a little something back for me, and that when the time was right, I'd get it.

Turned out it was a $50,000 life insurance policy. Inside the locked metal box that contained the policy along with the rest of her important papers, was a registration form for a modeling/acting school located in Philadelphia, just a little over an hour from where we lived at the time.

I knew what she had done. She didn't want me working behind the cosmetics counter at the mall for minimum wage anymore; she wanted me to have better than that. Better than what she had. No matter how I'd come to be, my mother loved me more than she'd ever loved herself.

I smooth my chestnut brown hair in back, and then check my make-up one last time in the lighted vanity mirror and nod. Every hair is in place; my eyebrows tweezed into perfectly shaped arches, make-up flawless.

Preston is out front of my apartment by now, waiting impatiently to take me to the airport.

I have decided to go to Belize this holiday season. It is one of the tropical places I haven't visited on any of my 'holiday vacations' as Preston refers to them.

I've packed quite a bit more in my three suitcases this year. I hope that Preston won't bitch too much when the doorman of my apartment building loads them into the trunk of his Mercedes. It's not as if he has to load them, but still, he will be the one to unload them once we reach the airport.

I slide into the passenger side, leaning over and dutifully kissing him on the lips.

"How long are you staying?" he asks, with a rare smile crossing his lips. "You have a credit card at your disposal you know?"

I smile over at him just as I am expected to do.

"I only packed the bare necessities, love," I respond. "I'll be gone for nearly a month you know, and I don't like to take advantage of your generosity. You do too much for me, Preston. I don't deserve all that you lavish upon me."

His eyes flicker over me as he pulls his Mercedes from the curb into traffic, momentarily quiet. "If I didn't know better, I might think that you're trying to pick an argument with me. Have I ever begrudged you anything? Have I ever nit-picked your use of the credit cards that I've provided to you?"

"Of course not," I answer quickly. "I'm being totally sincere, Preston. I'm not going to see you for a month, and I certainly don't want to part on a bad note."

He nods and the quiet envelops us once again.

As we pull into the busy airport access road he breaks the silence. "See that you behave yourself. I'll have people watching."

"Don't I always?" I ask, turning my gaze to look him squarely in the eye. "Haven't you always received stellar reports on my comings and goings during my holiday vacations?"

He gives me a sardonic smile that isn't without a hint of warning. "Yes my lovely, you've always behaved appropriately. Still, I feel the need to reiterate this with you. Blame my own insecurities. You're such a rare find that I want to make sure you're always mine."

"And I want to make sure of the same," I reply, taking my left hand and gently caressing his handsome cheek. "I aim to please."

And with that our conversation ends until we reach the short-term parking. He escorts me inside the terminal, making sure that I have my First-Class boarding pass for the seat that he's pre-selected for me. It is Seat 2A as always. Seat 2B will remain empty throughout this flight and my connecting one as well.

Preston always makes it a point to purchase two adjoining seats in first class, not that he ever travels with me on these trips; he simply wants to make sure that no one sits next to me on these flights. He can't take the chance that it will be another man; one that might charm me away from him.

He hands me my carry-on and I lean in to kiss him once again on the lips as we reach the first class blow-through for security.

He pulls back quickly, not one for public affection. "Have a safe trip, Rian. I hope you enjoy your vacation."

"Happy holidays," I murmur, kissing him one final time and then watching him shift uncomfortably. "I'll miss you."

And with that, he turns on his heel and exits the terminal. I take a deep breath, and close my eyes momentarily, hoping like hell my plan is a good one.

Hopefully, if the gods are with me, and the plans I've put into motion months before are foolproof; I might choose not to return in January as expected. And if so, I will be free of Preston Barringer the second's possessive and controlling nature for good.

God willing.

Chapter 1

I stretch out languidly on the padded chaise that I claimed just outside my cabana at the Bay Breeze Resort in San Pedro. The location is perfect; the white-sand beach is pristine and located near a gorgeous barrier reef. The warm, sunny, salt-kissed breeze ripples soothingly through my hair.

I prop a leg up, lowering my sunglasses as I gaze down the long stretch of deserted beach. This is Day Three. This is *the* day.

Now what?

Why am I so uptight, so nervous?

I know the reason. Taking risks isn't in my nature. I've convinced myself that personal and financial security are at the top of my hierarchy of needs. After all, my mother literally died so that I would have financial security and now that I do, why in the hell am I walking a tightrope, in stilettos, over it?

Because it's not enough, and it's never been enough and I'm tired of rationalizing that it is, and that it should be.

It's why I carefully crafted a plan of my own for this holiday vacation. It has taken months, but every piece has fallen into place just the way it was supposed to.

Let's rewind, shall we?

I met Janell back in the summer at the country club. Yes, Preston makes sure that I have a membership at his club, which I know sounds extremely generous, but you have to understand, he spends a great deal of time there in the summer. He plays golf and tennis, watches his youngest child's swim meets, and then there *are* the poker games in the clubhouse with his cigar club.

He likes for me to spend time at the club during the days that he's there so that I'm available for the random hook-ups we have in secret places.

You see, the main clubhouse is an auspicious mammoth stone fortress that dates back to the pre-Prohibition days. It served its purpose back then mainly because of its numerous secret rooms and underground caverns where the contraband was hidden from government agents that were on a witch-hunt for those violating the law of Prohibition.

Preston knows every nook and cranny of the gothic mansion including the underground tunnels that lead to the long-deserted distilleries that were used to produce illegal spirits back in the day.

He told me one time as a young boy, he and his brother had discovered them. They used to explore them thinking they were some ancient catacombs that no one else knew about.

It's difficult for me to imagine Preston as a curious and mischievous child, because the one that I know is serious and brooding most of the time. He's direct and no-nonsense in a quiet yet intimidating way.

And very controlling.

But you've already guessed that, haven't you?

You need to know that his controlling ways have never reached the point of being abusive; I need to make that perfectly clear. His generosity with me is boundless, yet emotionally he gives me nothing of himself. My attempts at showing him affection are becoming rare these days, mostly because they've been ignored or have gone unappreciated in the past.

Now back to my plan.

Janell is a friend, but more than that, she is someone that I *trust* implicitly. She works the cocktail lounge at the club in the summer, and during the off-season months, as a bookkeeper for her father's restaurant.

What's interesting about Janell is that she's roughly the same age as me, and the same height and build. So, with sunglasses, and a chestnut brown wig that is styled like my hair, she can easily pass as me to even the most discerning eye.

Yes, Preston hires locals to check up on me during my holiday vacations. I didn't realize it at first, but by the end of the second holiday trip, I had pretty much figured it out for myself. Don't get me wrong, they keep their distance of course, and try to blend in with other tourists, but you might be surprised how boredom can serve to sharpen one's senses and increase awareness.

When I asked Preston about it he didn't deny it. He didn't even feel sheepish or embarrassed about it. Why should he? It is his inborn sense of entitlement that makes doing something like this perfectly reasonable in his mind.

So, therein a plan was hatched--and the very reason for the additional luggage was to provide Janell with recognizable clothing to wear for digital pictures that most likely would be text messaged back to Preston periodically.

Once my flight landed, I caught up with her outside of the airport. She had been booked on an earlier flight. I left the additional suitcase that I'd packed with my clothing in it for her to wear beside a bench near the cab stand where she sat reading a magazine, and pretending to be oblivious to me.

Without a word I head down the sidewalk and hire a cab to drive me to San Pedro, while she heads to the resort in Belize City for the duration of her free holiday vacation.

I simply love it when a plan comes together without a hitch. But don't think that a lot of preparation and hard work didn't go into this in advance.

Janell is well versed in the food that I typically order, the cocktails I drink, and even the choice of books I download to my tablet, which she has with her.

You see, she is staying at the resort that I booked and charged to my credit card; the one that Preston pays off each month, under my name in Belize City. She even has my written signature down to perfection. I know because I was relentless making her practice it over and over again until she got it right. Then I teased her that she could make a killing in the forgery business. But she is simply happy to get a well-deserved, tropical vacation at no cost to herself.

I, on the other hand, carefully and methodically stashed away money all summer. I was able to return charged items for cash after Preston paid off the credit card balance each month.

Pretty savvy, huh?

With the cash I received from the returns, I purchased pre-paid Visa cards to use during this trip, but I won't be staying in Belize City. You see, I'm going to San Pedro, where I've booked my own accommodations under another name. Once in San Pedro, my name will no longer be Rian Thomas--for a while anyway.

In San Pedro, I am Presley Patterson from Baltimore, Maryland, and I am finally going to meet the man that I've been chatting with for almost a year now. We actually met in one of those online chat rooms. I have a secret laptop that Preston doesn't know about.

Okay, so chill for a minute.

It's not as if he wouldn't *allow* me to have a laptop, because he most definitely would buy one for me if I asked. He's not *that* much of a control-freak. But the thing is, it would simply be one more thing that he could monitor if he so chose and well, I need some privacy, all right?

So, I generally *act* as if the internet holds no interest for me, when the truth is that the ole' information highway is what has kept me *sane* over the past couple of years. It's the bridge that takes me from lonely to alive, from quiet and reserved, to funny and social--all the things that I'm afraid to be around Preston.

'Afraid' might not be the appropriate word here. I'm not *really* afraid of Preston; it's just that I feel it's my responsibility to please him. So, being funny, social and totally uninhibited are probably not what he *expects* from me, but I'm finding out slowly and surely that it is who I am--or at least, who I *want* to be. It feels natural and real.

Not fake.

Not the way that I am around Preston. Around him I am quiet and reserved, and I do what is expected of me.

Always.

Chapter 2

I'm back inside my cabana, freshly showered and dressed provocatively for bed. I thought this day would never end, because the anticipation of finally meeting *him* is running through my veins like hot, molten lava at the moment.

My nerves are wreaking havoc right now and suddenly, I'm filled with apprehension and those same old self-doubts come creeping in. They're every bit a part of me as my chestnut brown hair, or my size 34C breasts, or my allergy to penicillin. I am full of uncertainties about why the hell I am here. My self-confidence is nil.

My mind is tossing around questions that I can't answer.

What if he doesn't show?

What if this is some monumental, practical joke on his part?

I calm myself, my inner voice convincing me that Nathan *will* show, just as we've been planning for all of these months. He is sweet and kind, and he cares about me. He understands my situation and doesn't pass judgment on it although he's made it clear to me that he feels I deserve more--so much more.

Nathan is twenty-nine years-old, single, works as an investment counselor for a firm in Chicago. We've described ourselves to one another--just the basics, but have never actually exchanged pictures.

The reason being that we've both agreed that *whatever* we've become to one another is *not* founded on physical appearance, but based totally on what we've come to know about one another, and how we each feel about the other.

There's nothing superficial about our relationship. At this point, I don't give a rat's ass if he has a friggin' hump on his back as long as he shows up as planned.

I've shared with Nathan everything about my past-- things I've shared with no one else. He knows the story about my mother and the circumstances leading up to my becoming a model. He knows everything about Preston as well and what I am to him. He doesn't care.

I relax, telling myself that if the truth has scared him off--or turned him off, he wouldn't have come up with the plan to meet up with me over the holidays. It was totally his idea, and *that* fact alone finally convinces me that he'll be here as planned.

I make sure the door to my cabana is unlocked, and that the exterior light is on. That is in the plan.

I think about the things that he's shared with me, too. No deep dark secrets, mostly the typical frustrations of working in corporate America, with the added pressure of managing financial portfolios for demanding clients. He works ten-hour days, skips lunch and works out every evening at the gym. I know this much from his chats with me.

I have no clue about his social life, because well---it's none of my business and because I've become so enamored with him, that I prefer not knowing. There's nothing I can do about it anyway. I never ask personal questions of him, but I don't mind answering the ones that he asks me. I love that he's interested in my life, my thoughts and my feelings. He has this uncanny ability to literally read between the lines of my messages to him, picking up on my moods--good, bad or in-between.

Finally, near eleven o'clock, I'm worn out from thinking about it, plus the worry and apprehension are finally ebbing so I crawl up onto the huge bed with the nylon netting surrounding it and wonder what he will feel like.

What will his voice sound like?

I've pictured him in my mind a thousand times, but no matter what his physical appearance, I know that I won't be disappointed because I love his mind.

And his heart.

I love the story he messaged me a few months back about the stray dog he found one rainy morning on his way to work. He turned around and went back to get it, coaxing it into his car, and taking it back to his 'No Pets Allowed' apartment where he dried it off, and fed it anything he could find suitable for a dog. He was late for work, but he didn't care. He still has the dog. And he calls him 'Dingo.'

Sometimes I'm amazed at the way that he cares about me, without really knowing me. His words can pick me up in a heartbeat when I'm feeling down or particularly lonely. He has the ability to pull information out of me the same way a magician can wave his magic wand and pull a rabbit from his hat.

I think these thoughts as I let out a sigh, and roll over so that I can turn out the bedside lamp. I sink back and settle into the downy softness of my bed. A breeze trickles through the slatted shutters, and caresses my skin gently. My body is barely covered in the thin, black satin nightie that I selected for tonight. It is pitch black out tonight. Even the stars and moon are hidden by the thick cloud cover over the water. It's a perfect night for us.

Sleep finally overtakes me.

Minutes, or maybe it's hours later I'm awakened when I feel the bed dip down beneath someone else's weight, but I'm not frightened, and the fact that I'm not surprises me.

But I know who it is, and I feel the smile spread across my lips. "You're here," I whisper, feeling his warmness next to me.

"Did you ever have any doubts?" he responds, his voice is deep and husky, just like I imagined it would be.

"A few," I replied, because honesty is what we did, he and I.

"Silly girl," he says, and I can smell his musky scent. His skin touches mine and his fingers trace a slow, gentle trail up my leg to my thigh and I deliciously shiver.

"God I want to see you," he whispers, "Your skin is so soft and you feel so fucking beautiful and I need to see for myself."

"Remember our pact," I remind him softly. "This is the only chance we'll have to envision one another by touch alone. Do you really want to spoil that?"

He lets out a low growl, but I can feel his smile as he scoots closer, hovering over me.

My hands frame his face, and in total darkness I can feel a bit of stubble on his cheeks. He's got some five o'clock shadow going on which immediately puts some points into his column.

My fingers trace his lips, which are full and sensual, and as they travel along his jaw line, they reach his chin which I'm pleased to say has a dimple right there in the center.

Oh God! I love chin dimples . . .

"My turn, Presley," he whispers gently.

Okay, yeah . . . we share honesty except for names; but that's okay because Nathan isn't his real name either. We both know this much.

I close my eyes, losing myself to his touch. I can feel the slightly calloused pads of his fingertips gently touching my face, in different places, tracing along my jaw line, before they lightly caress my cheeks. He slowly moves over my nose, and then ever so lightly brushes the arch of my brows, taking his time, letting out a sigh as he finishes.

"You're beautiful," he murmurs, huskily, and I can feel his warm breath against my skin as he says it. "You're fucking beautiful," he repeats.

He leaves my lips for last, slowing his exploration so that he touches every centimeter of them.

"I want to kiss them," he breathes and I feel my skin tingle in response.

"Go ahead," I murmur, keeping my eyes closed.

And I feel his soft, full lips claim my own very gently, with a calm and deliberate sensuality. I'm expecting rougher, more possessive kissing from him because that's what I'm used to with Preston, but he doesn't. He has a totally different manner about him and I like it.

But it is foreign to me, so I'm not sure I can trust it.

"Relax," he instructs me, and I realize that I have grown tense and I'm not sure why. Am I cheating on Preston? Is that even possible?

"Don't think about him," he says; his tone now brusque. "This is about you and me, nobody else, okay? We're both where we want to be, and for this moment in time, no one else exists but the two of us."

"I'm sorry," I stammer, feeling my face flush with a little bit of shame and a touch of embarrassment. He totally gets me, and not only that, but he's able to sense my unspoken emotions. He even recognizes that I have them. I want to clutch him closer to me, but I'm clueless as to how he might respond, or what he might think.

Will he feel my desperation?

Probably.

The truth is that I *am* desperate. Desperate to be held closely within his strong and safe arms, and to be cherished and loved--not just fucked at someone else's leisure.

That's what Preston does. He fucks me; he doesn't make love to me. And I'm not saying that he doesn't fuck me well, because he does most of the time, but my orgasms (when I have them) are simply a coincidence; they're never a result of his expertise, or concerted effort on his part. It's all about him when we fuck.

And now it's no longer enough. It hasn't been since Nathan and I first chatted in that room - that internet room called "Owners of a Lonely Heart."

Always on my guard, I hadn't opened up to him much at the start, but somewhere along the way he'd earned my trust, and I his. Soon after, I found myself looking forward to getting online and going to our chat room to meet him. We even kept weekly schedules of when we'd be in the room.

Occasionally, I would have to miss a 'chat date' with him because of Preston's demands. Afterwards I would sense a cold aloofness in his messages, and I know that sounds weird, but it's the truth.

So, I finally broke down and explained the entire situation to Nathan, deciding that if I lost his respect because of it, then better to know now rather than later, when I might be more emotionally invested.

What a crock of shit. It was apparent that I'd become invested almost immediately with him. There had just been something--something unique and special in the way that he approached me. I sensed a sort of vulnerability in him, much like my own when it came to matters of the heart.

And now his soft, full lips are working mine with a gentle determination and we fit perfectly. I loop my arms around his strong neck and pull him closer; savoring the feel of his body, and his natural scent permeates my senses.

His tongue traces my bottom lip, and his teeth nip gently at it, teasing the way for his tongue to find mine. Our rhythm is perfect and I melt against him, giving a half-sigh, and half-moan at finally being able to touch and taste this man who's been my total distraction for a better part of a year now.

"I've dreamed of this," he growls softly, brushing my hair back with his hand, and moving his lips to the column of my neck, lazily kissing and tracing the sensitive skin with his tongue.

God, I so want to see his face, because I've imagined it a hundred times, but we agreed we would wait until afterwards. We wanted to meet in the dark of night, and then see one another in the morning light.

Sounds like a poem, doesn't it? A strange one at that.

Maybe so, but this is how we decided it would be.

His hand explores further down, gently moving the spaghetti strap of my nightie over my shoulder, then moving to the other side to do the same. I wriggle free of it, wearing nothing but a silk thong.

I can feel his hardness against me as he lowers his weight back down onto me, and I'm glad he came to me shirtless because the feeling of his chest against mine has me totally wet.

My fingernails trace his broad, muscular shoulders, moving downward on his back, loving the feel of his skin underneath them. He moves his lips from mine, and lowers his head to my breasts, where his tongue expertly teases the nipples into hard nubs.

I'm tingling now, every nerve in my body from scalp to toes is responding to this man and to everything he's doing to me. He suckles hard on a breast, and I let out a soft moan, writhing underneath him in exquisite pleasure.

"Easy," he says, his hand now moving lower as his lips brush across my sternum to the other breast. "I want to take this slow, baby. I want to love every part of your body with mine. I want to touch every inch of you with my lips and my tongue, and when you come, I want to taste it."

"Mmm," is the only response I'm capable of giving at the moment, because I'm consumed by him. I want his mouth back on mine and I whimper until he understands and moves his lips back up to mine, capturing them roughly this time. Our tongues meet in a mating ritual that is ours alone.

I feel like a savage as my mouth claims his with total abandonment, my teeth nipping at his bottom lip, tugging at it, but it feels real and honest for a change.

His fingers are moving lower, tracing an intricate pattern on my skin that leaves me breathless. With one swift movement on his part, my thong becomes history, but I don't care. His fingers travel to my apex, and my pussy is wringing wet for him.

Only him.

"I love your scent," he whispers huskily to me, dipping a finger inside and moving it sensually within me. My hips roll in pleasure and he withdraws it. "Mmm," he moans softly, and I hear a suckling sound. "You taste so fucking good, too. I might just want to suck on your pussy all night."

I tingle beneath his touch; my sensitive skin warms as his fingers return to tenderly ply the soft folds of my sex apart once more to begin his sensual, slow exploration. I feel my sharp intake of breath as he gently squeezes my swollen clit between two fingers.

I feel his smile against my lips.

"Your pussy is so sweet and so wet, baby. Is that just for me?"

"Yes," I whisper hoarsely.

And I gasp as he pushes his finger back inside of me, and then another, while his thumb rolls over my clit sending shock waves to my spine. My hips roll in response to his fingers fucking me. He knows exactly how to curl them up and then straighten them out to hit my very special spot that quickly becomes engorged. Another whimper escapes me as I press my hips upward so that his palm is pressed hard against my pubic bone.

"Patience, Presley," he murmurs, removing his fingers from me. God, I want to scream!

Is he punishing me?

I hear him chuckle, once again, reading my emotions--or possibly my mind.

He moves downward, and in the darkness of the cabana, I'm able to feel his warm breath between my trembling legs. His tongue laves my wetness as if he's drinking in some sweet nectar, sucking gently on my bud, and teasing it with his teeth.

Oh God.

His fingers return to the mix, deliberately fucking me with his skilled expertise. I feel as if I'm ready to explode.

"Come for me, baby."

And I do.

But this orgasm is like none before. The buildup is so intense that when I finally succumb to it, I feel a burst of wet release pour from me as wave after wave of pleasure rocks every nerve ending inside of me. Moaning his own pleasure, he laps every last drop of my sweet nectar as it comes from me and I am amazed at what I've just experienced with him. I've never climaxed wet before; I never knew it was possible and I am in total awe of this man's effect on me.

I haven't even touched his cock yet.

I release a loud sigh; my post-climax skin is sensitive and goose-bumped, and I relax back against the soft pillows. I'm satiated and it's totally because of him.

"Oh, we're not even close to being done," he whispers in my ear. I shiver.

"I want to see your cock," I blurt, and immediately feel my face flush.

What is up with that?

I never use words like that in bed.

Ever.

I hear his soft chuckle. "Remember our pact," he reminds me. "But you'll feel it tonight, baby. All night long if you can keep up, that is."

"Is that a challenge, Nathan?"

"Are you up for it?" he asks.

"The question is are *you* up for it?"

"Game on, baby."

Chapter 3

My eyes flutter open, drinking in the sun-kissed morning light that is now seeping in through the wooden slats of the window. I stretch lazily, and arch my back with feline grace. It takes a moment for me to get my bearings, and when I do, I sit up in bed quickly.

I look around the room frantically--searching for *him*. But I'm alone and my mind races to put the puzzle pieces into some semblance of order.

He was here. I'm sure of that. It's not possible that I dreamed *everything* that happened here--in this bed last night.

Is it?

I peer under the sheets and release a sigh as I see my nakedness. I peer over the edge of the bed, my eyes locking on the ripped thong and satin nightie pooled together on the floor where he'd discarded them. Beside them, three torn condom wrappers are scattered about. But it seems to me, in my morning haze, that we had fucked so much more than just three times.

Bits and pieces of what transpired the previous night in this bed under a cloak of darkness flash through my mind, like some Power Point presentation. Hard-muscled limbs entangled with mine; lips and tongue that hungrily and expertly work magic all over me, sending shock wave after shock wave through every nerve in my body.

His warm breath on my damp skin, murmuring words to me that bring shivers of delight and anticipation upon me. His intentions are made perfectly clear as he outlines everything he wants to do to me, and I'm already wet again.

His cock, hard and rigid, my hand curls around it, bringing it closer to me, wanting it inside of me. Wanting nothing more than him to possess and claim me as his. Sounds primal but that's how I felt.

And then his soft chuckle when he lifts me up as if I weigh nothing, and settles me down onto his sheathed cock.

His fullness takes my breath away. My body takes him inside of me, and my hips instinctively start a mating rhythm with his, our breathing becomes faster as our thrusting becomes deeper and harder.

Soft moans and feminine mewling, along with the wet fucking sounds our bodies are making together fill the room. He groans in pleasure as my pussy contracts around his girth, and he tells me to keep fucking him just like that.

And I do. I ride his cock up and down, my hands squeezing his balls ever so gently as I feel him nearing climax. Then I lean over just a bit, so that the head of his dick is hitting my sweet spot over and over again. I want us to come together.

And we do. We both come and cry out as wave after wave of orgasmic pleasure spirals through our joined bodies.

Afterwards we are left breathless; our bodies are damp with perspiration and the smell of sex permeates the room. He draws me up beside him, his fingers gently lifting a damp lock from my shoulder so that his lips can place soft butterfly kisses on my throat and neck until I shiver again. He murmurs words of love to me and my heart swells at hearing them. A single tear spills from my eye, as I can't recall ever having felt this way before.

We rest.

I taste him; he tastes me and then we make love.

We rest.

We fuck.

We sleep tangled up together.

It must have been because I have never slept so soundly or contentedly, that I didn't hear or feel him leave me, leave our bed.

I pull the sheet up under my chin and bite my lower lip. I'm totally confused.

Why *did* he leave?

I glance around the room again trying to find some sign other than the condom wrappers on the floor that he was here.

But there is nothing, not a single note.

Panic starts to seep in. I throw the sheets back and leap from the bed, grabbing my robe from the closet and quickly putting it on. The bathroom is empty, but the toilet seat has been left up, a sure sign that a man has been here.

In the living room, everything is as it should be; nothing is out of place. I go to the door and see that it's now locked. I open it up, and take several steps outside so that I can scope out the deserted stretch of beach. There is nothing. There is no one.

Not even traces of footprints are left in the wet sand along the beach next to the water's edge.

I turn around and return to my cabana. Confusion overwhelms me as I draw a bubble bath for myself.

As I soak my thoroughly fucked and thoroughly loved body in the warm sudsy bubbles, I replay the chain of events of the night before over and over again in my mind.

It was perfection. There had been nothing said or done that would've caused him to be angry with me.

I convince myself that he likely went back to his place to shower, shave and change clothes. Maybe he's even going to surprise me by returning with breakfast; fresh strawberries with cream, warm croissants with butter and jam, and plenty of hot coffee to perk us up for the day ahead.

I smile and hum softly as I dress for the day, carefully applying make-up so that I look perfect for him. I brush my hair up into a ponytail and give myself a nod of approval. I pray he's not disappointed with what he sees.

The clock in the bedroom reads nine-thirty. My stomach has butterflies as I await his return.

∞

The clock in the bedroom reads nine-thirty.

P.M.

He's not coming back. As much as I've tried to rationalize his absence each hour that crawled slowly and painfully by today, my inner voice became louder and louder until the reality was deafening.

My stomach is empty. No butterflies. No tingling. No food. No appetite.

I crawl into my bed, and feel totally repulsed by the lingering scent of our sex that remains on the sheets.

Stupid me.

I hadn't allowed the housekeeping staff in today because I'd been sure that Nathan would be popping back in at any moment.

I make a mental note to call them first thing in the morning to change the sheets and thoroughly clean the cabana so there will be no remnants left of our night spent together.

He has wrecked me and then left the pieces behind so that I am forced to wallow in them for the rest of my holiday vacation. I never should've forgotten how very fortunate I am to have Preston looking after me, taking care of me, and providing the security that I need. Despite the total misery and humiliation I'm feeling right now, the silver lining in this cloud is the reinforcement of knowing that I still have my life with Preston. I feel ashamed of myself for putting it at risk.

Preston will never leave me in pieces.

As I curl up on my side, I draw my knees up under my chin and wrap my arms around them. I fall asleep in the fetal position, tears and sobs wracking the same body that he had made his, only the night before.

Chapter 4

The rest of my holiday vacation is spent inside of the cabana, mostly in the bed now made up with fresh sheets that smell of fabric softener--not passion or sex.

I'm in this self-imposed prison. I don't go outside to enjoy the sunshine, or to sink my bare feet into the warm, moist sand, or even to breathe in the fresh, salty air.

I spend my days staring at the ceiling, and counting the number of revolutions the ceiling fan completes per minute, per hour until dusk settles in and I go to the refrigerator and pull out an apple or some of the withered grapes that are still there to take in some nourishment before the day is blessedly over.

I'm punishing myself for the stupidity I allowed to govern me, for the emotions and curiosity I had no right to feel, but mostly for my lack of good judgment in putting what I have--what I should be grateful for--at risk.

How could I be so unappreciative of all that Preston has given me? How could I possibly want more than I already have? I'm not bound to him by the chains of matrimony; I'm free to leave anytime I wish.

But why would I want to?

He gives me all that I need. He takes care of me in almost every way possible. He provides the financial and emotional security that my mother never enjoyed.

She struggled, always worried that she couldn't provide enough for me; or that my future wouldn't be secure.

Having seen this firsthand, I never wanted to struggle the way that she had. Having children wasn't part of my plan--I saw the stress and anxiety it had caused for my mother. I wanted no part of that.

It dawns on me that the very thing my mother had tried to instill in me--a sense of my own independence--was absent. As much as she had tried, I simply wasn't that person, nor could I ever be. She had taken care of me, sacrificing herself in the process.

I hate that I've failed her; but after all, I *am* my mother's daughter. And like her, my livelihood is secured at the whim of a man, not *men* as was her case, but if I'm lucky, I will fare much better than she had.

I am resolute in making sure that Preston remains content with me, and to never again put myself at risk.

∞

I spot Preston at the bottom of the escalator waiting for me. He seems anxious to see me. Our eyes lock, and I quickly plaster a smile on my face, waving to him.

He smiles but it doesn't reach his eyes; it almost never does.

As I step off of the escalator, his eyes flicker over me as if he's inspecting his merchandise for damage.

This is new.

"Welcome home, Rian," he says softly, reaching for me.

I'm stunned because Preston typically does not show affection publically--or even *privately* for that matter. It's usually only done in bed under the guise of fucking.

But I go with it, dropping my bag to the floor and putting my arms around him as he squeezes me against his chest. "Have you lost weight?" he asks, pulling back to get a better look at me. He seems concerned.

"I don't think so," I reply, wondering how in the hell he can tell with my winter coat buttoned up tightly around me. I know that I have lost weight, though I'm just not sure how much.

"Have you been ill? You never mentioned it in your text messages back to me."

"I'm fine, Preston," I sigh. "I'm just glad to be home."

∞

We stop for dinner on our way back to my apartment from the airport. Preston insists that I order dessert after my meal having seen and commented once again about my obvious weight loss.

"Didn't you enjoy Belize?" he asks, giving me his full attention now, waiting for my response.

"It was okay, I guess. Maybe next Christmas I'll go somewhere with snow."

"We have snow here," he deadpans. "I thought the whole point was for you to get *away* from the snow and enjoy warm weather in the winter."

"That's just it," I reply thoughtfully, "I need to learn to appreciate the snow, and not try and escape it. Snow is the reality of where we live, isn't it?"

"You sound unusually pragmatic," he retorts. "What bit of wisdom crossed your path?"

I shrug and give him a pensive smile. "I suppose these holiday vacations provide me with enough time to be introspective, and to get a dose of reality while I'm at it. It helps me appreciate what I have, Preston. I've missed you."

He smiles and nods, snapping his fingers for the server to bring him the check.

Once back at my apartment, he wastes no time in helping me out of my clothes.

"I've missed you as well, Rian," he murmurs, fisting my hair in the back and pulling me up against him. His lips ravage mine furiously and I know that we will be making up for lost time.

He quickly pulls me upstairs to my bedroom, and sheds his clothing immediately. His thick cock strains against his boxer shorts that remain in place.

"Come here," he instructs.

I walk across the thick carpeting to stand before him. His eyes are searching mine.

For something--though I'm not sure what.

Do I look different?

Does he sense . . . *something*?

"Tell me what you want?" he asks boldly.

This is new.

"I . . . I want you, Preston," I stammer in a quiet voice. "Always you."

"No. Tell me what you want at *this* moment."

I flush with confusion. I'm not sure what he wants to hear. I decide to go with instinct.

"I want your cock. I want you to bury your cock balls-deep inside of me."

He smiles wryly. "Do I need a condom?" he asks.

I'm stunned by the question, but pray that I'm not showing it. Preston and I never use condoms.

There's no point.

He's had a vasectomy and up until this point, I've never been sexual with anyone else other than him since that very first time. There's no way he could've known about the one night with Nathan. Besides that, we used condoms.

Based on his claims that his wife is rarely in the mood, my presumption has always been that we're practicing safe sex. If that has now changed, then he is the one to answer that question. Not me.

I face him squarely. "You tell *me,* Preston. Do *you* need a condom?"

Our eyes lock and I refuse to show anything less than honesty. There's no way that I'll break eye contact first with him. The ball is in his court now.

He remains silent, but his gaze is still penetrating. I don't back down. He moves closer, placing his hands on my shoulders and gently nudges me downward. I sink to my knees before him; my face is aligned with his bulging cock, still straining against the cotton material to be freed.

"Suck me," he says in a hoarse whisper. "Show me what your mouth can do."

I draw him out. I hear his sharp intake of breath as my mouth closes over the head of his dick, and my hands grip and squeeze the bare cheeks of his ass. I pull him into me more deeply.

Preston likes it rough, and that's exactly how I'm giving it to him. My mouth assaults his shaft from tip to root, and then back again.

He moans his pleasure, his one hand resting against the back of my head to steady my rhythm to match his thrusting.

"That's it," he says, "Keep sucking me like that, Rian. You like this too, don't you?"

I moan my assurance, swirling my tongue around the tip, and gently nip the ridge of sensitive skin around the head of it with my teeth.

"Ahh," he breathes, "That's my girl. That's my Rian."

Suddenly he stops his thrusting and pulls me to my feet. His hands frame my face, pulling my mouth to his as his tongue searches for mine. We are caught up in a rhythm of passion that is new to me-- from him that is.

Something is different.

"Do you *appreciate* my cock?" he asks me.

"Yes, Preston. Of course I do."

"Do you love what it does for you?"

"Yes."

"Did you miss it?"

"I did."

His hands turn me around so that my back is now to him. I feel his hands on my hips guiding me forward towards the bed.

"I want to fuck you from behind," he says.

I get on my hands and knees and move to the center of the bed. I feel him behind me now; one hand steadying me while the other grips his erection. I'm already wet for him, but he gives me a courtesy finger-fuck to make sure that I'm well-lubricated to receive his girth.

And yes, his cock is big.

[But ladies, let's clear something up right here and now. The size of a guy's dick doesn't necessarily mean that it has inborn talent. So please don't think that guys with smaller dicks can't make your eyes roll back in your head, or propel you to cry out dirty, filthy things like some two-bit strumpet, because I'm sure that they can. It's just that I personally haven't had any experience with those of . . . smaller . . . girth. We clear on that?]

As soon as his fingers leave my core, I brace myself for the forceful thrust of his cock as he enters me. I mean, that's his usual style - the great, swift plunge.

But he enters me slowly now and I'm pleasantly surprised by this. He's being unusually gentle, inching his erection into me with slow deliberation and care. Both of his hands are now braced on my hips, gently rolling them in sync with his slow, methodical thrusting.

"Does that feel good Rian? Does *this* cock feel good in your pussy?"

I hesitate momentarily; Preston doesn't generally talk during sex. He's extremely talkative today however.

"Oh yes," I reply honestly. "It feels *so* good, Preston."

We work ourselves into a slow rhythm; he rocks in and out of me slowly, his momentum picking up just a notch as we continue at this pace. I dare to arch my back just a bit in order to allow the head of his cock to hit my sweet spot.

It's *perfect*.

I moan loudly as he continues hitting my spot; my breathing escalates and it feels so fucking good with him right now that I can't stop mewling my pleasure. I sound like a whore in heat, but I don't give a damn because it feels *just* that good. It's never been *this* good . . . not with Preston.

Something has changed.

With him?

Or with me?

I don't dare stop to analyze it because I'm quickening like a horny bitch and he's murmuring things to me.

Dirty things.

Sexy things.

This is a *first* for that as well.

"You like how this feels, don't you?" he rasps from behind me, his hands now gripping my ass cheeks firmly.

"God . . . yes. Please don't stop."

I'm afraid that he *will* stop his thrusting and I don't even know why that thought enters my mind because he's enjoying this every bit as much as I am.

I'm on the verge of a major orgasm and I feel his hand circle around from the back. His fingers are splayed and his thumb finds my swollen clit. I gasp audibly as he rocks in and out of me, pinging my g-spot each and every time with his cock, while he rolls my swollen clit between his thumb and forefinger, gently pinching it.

"Oh God," I moan loudly, feeling the spasms being released from deep within my core, "Please don't stop!"

He groans as he meets my orgasm with his own powerful one. Several thrusts later I feel him stiffen as his cock throbs within me and I'm overwhelmed with how much pleasure he's given me.

"You love what *my* cock gave you," he whispers hoarsely as my orgasm starts to wind down just as his is exploding inside of me.

"Tell me. I need to hear it."

"Yes," I answer, trying to catch my breath. "I fucking love what your cock gave me," I finish in a hoarse whisper.

My breathing remains ragged from the climactic exertion, and my skin is still tingling from the remnants of having every single nerve ending in my body electrified by

Preston's cock. I clench my muscles around him feeling the warm squirts of cum pulsating inside of my soaked pussy.

Preston's breathing finally slows down as he gives one last shudder and empties the last drops of his climax inside of my body.

He backs out of me, and I can feel the wetness of our joint orgasms as it drips from us. He collapses beside me on the bed, his breathing still fast and hard from the exertion. My legs feel wobbly, and I join him, damp skin meeting damp skin.

"Damn," he growls, pulling me close, his fingers combing through my damp locks of hair. "That was fucking epic," he says, throwing his other arm up and over his forehead in exhaustion. "Maybe I need to send your ass to San Pedro more often," he says with a playful tease in his tone.

This is *totally* different.

"Oh yeah? Why's that?" I reply smiling as I revel in this post-orgasmic glow. I am feeling grateful that things between us seem to be better than before.

"Because the welcome-home sex is just *that* awesome," he says, giving me a smack on the butt. "You wore this old man out."

I raise myself up on one elbow and trace a fingernail lightly over his chest. "After *that* how can you possibly refer to yourself as an old man?" I ask incredulously.

"You're right," he replies, "You keep me in shape. I won't ever let you go."

He rolls away from me, and launches his lean frame from the bed. "How about we share a shower and then share tales of our holidays with one another?" he asks, heading toward the bathroom. "We've got some catching up to do."

"Yeah, sounds good," I reply, getting up ready to follow him, feeling my brow furrow with confusion.

"Would you grab some clean clothes for me?" he asks, nodding towards the dresser in my bedroom where he keeps clean boxers, tee shirts, socks and sweats. "I'll get the shower going for us."

"Sure thing," I call back to him before he closes the bathroom door behind him. I'm distracted by the fact that he wants to share holiday vacation stories.

This is definitely new.

And weird.

It dawns on me that maybe Preston has made some sort of New Year's resolution on my behalf. I mean, we've been sexual for several years, but intimacy like this has always seemed to elude us.

I brighten at the thought that this just might be the turning point our relationship so desperately needs. I'm optimistic that things will be better than ever. And maybe, just *maybe* I'll finally get the intimacy and love that I crave.

Can any one person be *that* lucky?

I'm still thinking those thoughts as I gather clean clothes for the both of us and head back towards the bathroom, tripping over Preston's shoes.

I stoop to pick up his trousers that are pooled on the floor at the foot of my bed and his wallet falls out.

It's a new leather wallet. A Christmas gift no doubt from a member of his family, maybe even from his wife, Emily.

I drop the clean clothing onto the bed, and start to put the wallet back into the pocket of his trousers when something makes me stop.

I'm not a snoop by nature. Believe me; in the three years since I've assumed the role of Preston's mistress, I've never snooped through his pockets, or driven by his home, or phoned his house and hung up on whoever answered-- that is simply not my style.

I don't even ask him questions about his family. He shares bits and pieces of his life with me as he sees fit, and I don't ask for more than what he's willing to give. But something propels me in this instant to look in his wallet and I don't know why.

With a flick of my wrist the bi-fold wallet opens and I immediately see that there's a picture inside the clear plastic window. It is marked as "Christmas 2014" in script at the bottom.

It's Preston and his family all together over the holidays. I recognize Emily from the club, and his youngest daughter Simone who's around twelve leaning against Preston. I recognize her from the club as well. She's on the swim team. Next to Emily is their son Patrick, I presume, who attends a private high school. If memory serves me correctly, Patrick's a senior, which makes him seventeen I would guess.

But my eye catches the oldest son; the one Preston barely ever mentions who is standing on the outside in this photo. I pull the picture out of the plastic and turn it over. I recognize Preston's neat handwriting on the back.

Oh my God.

'Em, Simone, Patrick, and Ethan - Xmas 2014 - Playa del Carmen'

Playa del Carmen?

Preston and his family spent the holidays in *Playa del Carmen?* That's like six hours away from where I had been staying .... But only four hours from where I was *supposed* to have been staying . . .

I hurriedly flip the picture back over and study his oldest son, Ethan. I freeze on the spot, trying like hell to put these puzzle pieces in some logical order. I blink a couple of times, not sure why, but my eyes follow the lines of his very handsome face; the strong jawline that seems familiar, as do the full, sensual lips.

It's when my eyes lower to his chin that I realize there is no mistaking that chin dimple. My lips tingle at my own body's internal memory of having kissed him . . . there; of my tongue settling . . . there; of my finger tracing the stubble . . . there.

Dark shadowy images of my secret lover dance through my mind.

Nathan---Ethan?

Fuck.

But why?

He doesn't look any older than twenty-one or twenty-two. I try like mad to remember Preston's mentioning him before, but there is little I recollect.

Something about him attending college somewhere in the Mid-West; not coming home often, and having a falling out of some sort with him over his career path. I wish I could recall more, but I can't. Preston doesn't speak all that much of his children, and in particular, his oldest one.

I study the picture again and Preston's words come back to me.

"*You love what* my *cock gave you.*"

His son?

"*Maybe I need to send your ass to* San Pedro *more often.*"

He said 'San Pedro'--not *Belize* or *Belize City*.

Oh my God.

Had he made a quick detour to Belize City? Surely Janell would've contacted me by cell if something unexpected had happened while she was at the resort there.

Right?

My mind rewinds to the morning I met Janell outside of the airport at the designated spot to retrieve my extra suitcase. We hadn't spoken to one another as planned; because you never know who might've been watching. She looked well-rested, tanned and very happy by the looks of the smile on her face.

I need to call her at the earliest opportunity. I feel frantic now with confusion and apprehension.

"Rian," he calls out from the bathroom. "Are you coming?"

I put the picture back in its place, and hurriedly stuff the wallet back into the pocket of his trousers, letting them drop back onto the floor where he stepped out of them earlier.

I take a really deep breath, willing myself to relax so that he doesn't notice that I'm coming apart. I can't afford to show that to him.

"I'm coming, Preston," I call out. "Be right there."

And as I make my way to the bathroom, my mind is still a flurry of contradictions and excuses. I feel shaky, and I know I can't face him until I calm down and get rid of the guilt that I know I'm wearing like a mask.

I take another deep breath, and force myself to consider the worst case scenario, that being that he somehow knows what I've done.

Wouldn't he have mentioned it to me by now? Done something to show me that I hadn't gotten away with anything?

The reality of Preston sinks in and I chide myself for not realizing it sooner.

Regardless of what he may or may not know, I realize there's no way that Preston will ever divulge the truth to me. Nor will he ever call me out on anything that might make him look as if he hadn't been in control of the situation.

And why should he?

After all, Preston Barringer the second is *always* in control, everyone knows that ...

No one ever dupes this extraordinary man.

The reality of the situation seeps into my brain and has an immediate calming effect, just as a rush of dopamine infiltrates my senses.

All is well.

I reach the bathroom door suddenly feeling exhilarated that I have a man such as Preston taking care of me - seeing to all of my needs, not only financially, but emotionally as well. Letting me know where I stand with him.

"You keep me in shape I won't ever let you go."

I feel the smile form on my lips as I recall his words of only minutes ago.

I am *so* lucky to have him.

Epilogue

Two Months Later

I scoot my butt up to the edge of the examining table as Dr. Maxwell has requested at least three times since he took his seat on the rolling stool at the end of it

"Don't worry, I'll catch you if you fall," he teases, as he grabs the warm speculum from behind him. His nurse is standing next to him, and by the dour expression on her face, it is apparent that she's totally bored. Must get old for her.

Same shit, different day.

"Relax your legs," he instructs, "Just let them fall open."

As if.

"That's better," he says, now opening me up to take a look.

God I hate this.

The palm of his free hand presses flat against my abdomen, and he moves and puts pressure in several places, before he finally swabs my cervix and unclamps me. I finally release the breath I've been holding.

"All done," he says, slipping off his latex gloves, and tossing them into the trash can next to the wall. "Raise your left arm up over your head," he instructs, as he starts the breast exam. "That's good. Now the other, please."

I comply and within another twenty seconds, he's finished.

"Seems fine. You can sit up now," he says, holding his hand out for me to take as he helps me up. I'm clutching the paper sheet up around my breasts now, and watch as he studies my chart.

Just then there's a light tapping on the door. His nurse opens it, and the lab technician hands her a piece of paper. She glances at it and then hands it over to Dr. Maxwell.

"Thanks, Sherry," he replies, looking it over. She leaves the room.

"Well Rian, I think I can explain the spotting you've been experiencing in lieu of your normal menstruation."

It's cancer. I know it.

It's just how my luck runs. Preston and I have been closer than ever since the holidays. I'm not clear on what exactly transpired with him and his family, because that day at my condo, we never got around to discussing it.

Once I joined him in the shower that afternoon, there was no talking period. It was as if Preston couldn't fuck me enough that day - and for the days following it.

I had been so grateful for being able to stay under the radar with the stunt I'd pulled, that I had struck a bargain with God. I promised to never take what I had with Preston for granted again in exchange for him not finding out about what I had done.

I mean, yes, his actions that day were . . . *strange*, but then again, Preston is a complicated person. He hasn't gotten where he is by being a fool, and he certainly is a proven master of masking emotions, that is evident in all of his dealings whether business, social or personal.

After he had left my bed the following morning, I had wasted no time in pulling my secret laptop out of hiding, and promptly tossing it into the dumpster out behind the condominiums. I was resolute in my commitment to avoid all temptation. Besides that, I didn't want to know what happened. Sometimes being kept in the dark is the best possible scenario.

Ignorance is bliss.

Like right now, as I continue hearing Dr. Maxwell repeating my name, as long as I don't acknowledge him, then no devastating news can reach my ears.

"Rian," he says once again, his voice verging on a shout. "Are you okay?"

I look up at him, realizing I've let my paper sheet fall to my waist. "It's cancer, isn't it?" I ask quietly.

"You haven't heard a word, have you?"

I shake my head, my hands death-gripping the sides of the table, braced for the words that are to come once again.

"You're pregnant, my dear."

Worse than cancer.

Totally not possible.

"That's not possible," I whisper, my eyes widening. "Preston's had a vasectomy."

Dr. Maxwell takes a seat on his rolling stool, and scoots in front of me. "How long ago?"

"What?"

"How long ago did Preston have a vasectomy?"

I shrug. "Before we started our relationship, so at least four years ago," I reply.

"Well, vasectomies are 97% effective, but the real issue is whether or not he followed up with his post-op visit and had his sperm count verified. You'd be surprised how many men don't follow through with that," he said, shaking his head. "So, I suggest you ask him about that when you give him the news."

Give him the news?

I'm silent. My mind is blank. Dr. Maxwell picks up on my distress. "Rian, have you been sexually active . . . outside of your current relationship?"

I shoot him a look.

"I'm not trying to pry; I'm merely trying to help you sort this out."

"How far along am I?"

"Nine to ten weeks. We'll have a more definitive estimation once we do your first ultrasound at your next appointment; that is . . . uh . . . if you plan to continue with the pregnancy."

"Yes."

"Yes---you plan to continue with the pregnancy."

"No. Yes I was sexually active outside of my current relationship, but only once, and we used condoms."

I feel my face flush with the confession to the non-judgy doctor--at least he's supposed to be, I think.

"Well, condoms are only 85% effective, so of course the odds are more likely that this sexual partner is responsible for the pregnancy, but again, that also is contingent upon the number of times you engaged in sex using condoms. That percentage is skewed because of people that never use anything *other* than condoms and unreported factors. Again, *knowing* if your current partner ever completed his post-surgery sperm count analysis is the key, Rian."

Holy shit.

"I understand," I reply meekly. "I need time to think about this, Doctor Maxwell, to fully absorb this news and to figure things out."

"Of course," he says, standing up, and heading towards the door. "You may get dressed now. Why don't you schedule an appointment for two weeks out just to be on the safe side? If you need to cancel for some reason, well you always have that option."

"I will," I say, blinking back tears.

"Good luck," he replies, right before the door closes behind him.

I'm in a stupor.

A shocked stupor.

I manage to get my clothes back on, not realizing until much later that I have buttoned my blouse up all wrong. Later, after I've made a follow-up appointment for two weeks out as the doctor instructed. After I've started my car up in the frigid, late February weather, backing out of the parking space, and being oblivious to the fact that

Doctor Maxwell is watching me from behind the blinds of his office window.

Because if I *had* been aware, I would've buttoned my blouse up properly; I might have reconsidered making that follow up appointment, and I may have even noticed the doctor staring through the cracks in his blinds making sure that I was out of the building before he picked up the phone on his desk to make a call.

And I would never know that the call Doc Maxwell made was to one of his oldest friends from the club, and the man I was about to confess my infidelity to, how ironic. I had to tell Preston about the other man.

Epilogue-Preston's POV

I realize that you probably can't connect with me; that through Rian's eyes you see me as a cold and aloof man--a dispassionate person who only regards Rian as a possession. Someone who is used to getting what he wants, at any cost.

You're only partially correct.

I am a man who knows what he wants, and goes after it until it's mine, no argument there. But that's not to say that I don't *appreciate* what is mine, and that I don't take proper care of my possessions, because that is not accurate.

I don't regard Rian as a possession; people can't be owned, we all know that, but she is mine and I do see to her needs as best I can.

Do I love Rian?

Love is such a fleeting emotion, and despite those that will tell you differently, it isn't a static one, but rather a very dynamic one. As one experiences life and maturity, it is only natural that one's perspective of love transitions as well. And despite what you've been told, love is not unconditional. Anyone who insists that it is, well, they're full of shit.

Let's just say that I appreciate Rian very much. I respect her as a human being. And most importantly, I am grateful for Rian. It is not all about my needs or my pleasures or my agenda as you might be inclined to believe. Her happiness and contentment are paramount to me. Every bit as much as my wife's needs are important to me. No—that's not true. Rian's happiness is more important to me than my wife's and I think it's because of the fact that she is the polar opposite of Emily.

Rian is most likely the woman I would've wooed, romanced and taken to be my wife had I have had a choice in the matter. But that's not how things happen within the East Coast aristocracy that still exists.

So, you see, I don't take her for granted. We've been together long enough that I can sense when things are troubling her. Not that she is one to complain, because that simply isn't her style. Rian is appreciative of me, and sometimes I wonder how that can possibly be.

I'm a man who is not only keenly aware of, but has also ultimately come to terms with my emotional deficiencies and lack of affection when it comes to other human beings.

Maybe it's a result of having been born and raised in a family of wealth, where feelings were locked inside stone fortresses, and expression was not welcomed or appreciated.

As the oldest of two, my brother Landon being ten years younger than myself, I had received a decade's worth of instruction and reinforcement of exactly what my parents' expectations were for me before he had even arrived on the scene.

By the time he did, my parents were satisfied that I was well on my way to success, and it became obvious that I was the designated heir apparent, so Landon was off the hook. His formative years were less complicated as a result, and from all indications, much happier.

I can't complain. I've lived a life of wealth and opportunity, and those ideals and ethics ingrained in me at an early age, served to get me where I am today.

My brother Landon?

Yeah, he plays a lot of golf, takes family vacations and lives a much simpler life than I do. But that has more to do with birth order and less to do with choice.

Getting back to Rian, I understand what life has dealt her and it had been cruel. No matter how beautiful she is, in her own mind, it will never be enough. She's not so different than me in that respect. She's living out her mother's hopes and dreams for her--all well-meant of course, but not of her choosing.

Rian has settled, the same way that I have settled. But the thing is, I care enough for her and about her that I will do whatever I need to do to ensure that she's happy and content.

That means I not only have had to read between the lines of what she says to me, but I also have to dissect the unsaid, which is no easy task with her. She's simply not one to complain, or to appear ungrateful or unfulfilled. She doesn't play it that way, and never has.

So, now we get to the crux of my story. Nearly a year ago, I had sensed a subtle change in Rian's demeanor. Though she never verbalized it, her body language and her avoidance of discussing it had been my biggest clue.

And then there had been the secret computer she had purchased.

Yeah, that had been the most obvious signal of her detachment and discontent. She knew that there was no reason why she had to purchase anything secretly; all she had to do was buy it, and I paid the monthly credit card bill.

So obviously, there had been a reason why she made this particular purchase covertly. She must've purchased it from cash withdrawals made a little bit at a time. She knew damn well I would've questioned large cash withdrawals, because that is simply my nature.

I concluded that she must have had something she felt compelled to hide from me.

Oh, she had no clue that I knew about it, but part of my obsession with Rian had been to make sure I was always aware of what she was doing when I wasn't around.

I had inadvertently rifled through her bedside drawer one morning while she was in the shower, looking for nail clippers when I discovered the wireless hot spot. Since she had consistently refused my offer of a home computer, I found it odd.

The only electronics Rian owned were her smart phone and her e-reader, both of which were covered on my cell phone plan. Why then did she require a separate hot spot?

I had powered the device only to discover she had used 2 GB's of a 6 GB monthly plan. A plan she apparently had been paying in cash on her own.

Two days later, while Rian and I were out to dinner, one of my associates combed through her condo and discovered the secret laptop.

Within a day, I was tracking her internet movements and quickly discovered that my instincts had been on target. Rian was restless, lonely, unfulfilled in some incomprehensible way.

She had been visiting some on-line chat room called "Owners of a Lonely Heart." Looking for something, or maybe someone to make her life complete.

Of course, I had been dismayed at the idea of losing her, and it became apparent to me that I must somehow find a way to fill whatever void in her life had prompted this erratic behavior.

That is when I assumed the identity of "Nathan."

Yes, I am *Nathan*. The not quite thirty investment counselor at some bogus firm in Chicago. I'm purportedly living the dream of Corporate America, being too focused on my career, along with the stray dog I've adopted, to cultivate a relationship borne of an internet chat room with Prudence Patterson, Rian's pseudonym or alter ego, the latter being a more accurate description.

Pathetic?

It depends.

Are you referring to me or to Nathan?

I saw no harm in creating this persona, or alter ego if you prefer, in order to keep Rian company when her married lover could not. And yes, it was no surprise that in Rian's description of said lover, he came across as ambivalent and detached, and emotionally inattentive.

I actually found myself looking forward to our secret internet trysts. It offered me the rare opportunity of getting inside her head, and with Nathan, it became obviously apparent that she had no reservations about sharing her innermost thoughts and feelings.

And dreams. I became almost jealous of Nathan in that respect, as ridiculous as it sounds, because obviously, I was him, but still the fact that she opened up so much to a stranger was puzzling.

Had I always been so distant and aloof with her that she felt always on guard? Was I unapproachable? I thought back and realized that I had never encouraged her to open up about anything. I had never even entertained the notion that she may have insecurities or cause for concern where our relationship was concerned. I learned so much more about the woman I'd been involved with for more than three years as a stranger than as the active participant in the relationship. How sad and pathetic is that?

I can only blame myself. But there's time for that later, I suppose. Some of the things I learned have given me cause for concern.

You see, during some of these chats Prudence confided to Nathan that she had dreams of marriage, maybe even having a child or two. She talked of breaking things off with Preston, not only because she knew she would never have either of those things with him, but also because of people getting hurt and the wrongness of how she lived. It clearly tormented her and again, she had never shown any outward signs of this to me.

Nathan simply listened and consoled, never judging but being punished nonetheless by her words that were the sad truth that she couldn't--or wouldn't share with her lover.

I had printed out the chat conversations between her and Nathan, and I had studied them again and again, allowing her emotions to weep over me until finally I knew what had to be done.

I couldn't lose Rian. I loved her. But I'd never told her that because it was something I didn't do; I never had. Not with any woman, not even my wife, and until I became involved with Rian, I had held no certainty that love was an emotion that I would ever allow myself to feel.

But it couldn't be helped.

The heart wants what the heart wants, and yes, I know how pathetically trite and overused that sounds. I have no other way of explaining it though.

It wasn't because I couldn't say the words--that was the easy part; it was because up until this point, I had never felt like saying them. Not until the reality hit me that Rian might leave, that I could very well lose her, and that if that happened, I would have no one to blame other than myself.

My marriage was a business venture; a joining of portfolios if you will. Emily and I both understood that going into it because our families had been adamant that it was a merger made in heaven. Emily's family was old money. Her great-grandfather had been an entrepreneur, migrating to the U.S. through Ellis Island during the tail end of the second Industrial Revolution. He had held patents on seven different machine tools which had brought millions to the family coffers post World War I.

So, yes, money had been the driving force of our marriage, but that was the same impetus for my parents' marriage and her parents' marriage. It's not a unique thing among families of wealth on the East Coast.

And up until the day I had first seen Rian, I honestly hadn't strayed from my vows. There had been no reason to do so. Emily met my needs, and though I suspected that she had strayed a time or two during our years together, I hadn't been particularly bothered by it because she was discreet. And let's face it, I wasn't oblivious to the fact that she had emotional needs that weren't being met. I knew that, but hell, I believed it was simply a female characteristic: the need for intimacy, closeness, and attentiveness. That had been my own short-sightedness, my male macho perspective I guess.

Eventually, I learned that those human needs are not restricted only to females, the only difference being that man are reluctant to admit that they have the same need for emotional fulfillment. Yeah, I guess Rian put me in touch with my feminine side. That's about as humorous as I get, just so you know.

Okay, so now I'm just stalling because what comes next I'm sure that you will think is despicable of me, but rewind. Remember the two most important things you've learned so far about me:

- *I'm a man who gets what he wants, and I keep what I have.*

- *Rian is precious to me. I won't let her go, nor will I allow her to be unfulfilled or unhappy.*

So, having said that, and with all I've learned about Rian through the many cyber chats between *Prudence* and *Nathan* in "Owner's of a Lonely Heart," I set out to make sure that her needs were going to be met. Anything is possible when you love and treasure another human being.

I couldn't give her marriage. Clearly, that is out of the question for the reasons stated above. But perhaps I could help with the other dream she spoke about; she wanted to be a mother.

I had a vasectomy after the birth of our last child, Simone. Having a reversal isn't an option—not one that I even entertained. But there was another way.

Being the person that I am, and yes, controlling adequately describes it best, I am very much in tune with Rian's cycles. I also knew who I could approach, with nothing less than a hefty bribe and a bit of a threat tossed in for good measure to get the job done.

My oldest son, Ethan, and I have been estranged for several years. The reason for the estrangement is not important. Strike that, yes, it is important in a way I suppose. You see, Ethan is the product of an…indiscretion I had prior to my marriage to Em. We had been engaged for more than a year, and I was finishing up my Master's degree at Stanford. We were at opposite sides of the country, and I carried on a short term affair with a fellow student named Caroline.

To make a rather long---and painful story short, Caroline ended up pregnant and had no inclination to raise the child. I, on the other hand, did not want a scandal or some type of blackmail to surface later on down the road. I immediately confided my indiscretion to my father, and the family attorneys handled the legalities with respect to having Caroline sign over her rights to the yet unborn child.

Em was forgiving, but only because it was in her best interest to be so. She moved to the west coast, where we eloped. A year and a half later, we returned to Boston with our first born son, Ethan, for all to see and accept as being a product of our marriage.

The problem was that Em could never really accept him as her own, and that became even more apparent after the birth of Patrick and Simone. It was obvious to me, and eventually, it became obvious to Ethan.

He was sent away to a good boarding school at the age of twelve, and then onto college. Finally, while he was in college I was compelled to tell him the truth. It had angered him that I had waited so long to reveal something that I had hoped I would never have to explain to him.

He became even angrier when I had refused to reveal his birth mother's identity. We became estranged after that, and once I realized that Nathan might be the answer to the dilemma I had with Rian, I concocted a plan that would give him what he wanted, and also, to give Rian what she desired.

I approached Ethan with a plan. I divulged everything to him relative to my relationship with Rian. Of course, there was no love lost between Ethan and Em, so when I explained the full extent of what I needed from him, he had only minor hesitation before agreeing to it.

"What if it doesn't happen though?" he had asked.

"I will still hold up my end of the bargain," I had assured him. And with that, my son had agreed to travel to San Pedro and be "Nathan" for a night of passion with my Rian, and to hopefully, impregnate her with his seed. In return, I agreed to provide him with his birth mother's name, as well as her current location so that he could meet her which is all he had wanted.

To minimize as much risk as possible that Rian would not conceive over the holiday interlude, I had contacted her gynecologist, Dr. Maxwell, and set up a meeting with him. We knew each other well from the club. I knew his Achilles Heel: Money. The good doctor had a gambling problem that always seemed to have him by the wallet. So, I lined his pockets well, and in return, he provided me with a fertility drug to slip Rian which would maximize her chances of conception. Everything had been put into place.

Afterwards, when I picked her up at the airport, I had seen how much Nathan's swift and mysterious departure had affected her. I hadn't considered that in the scheme of things. Had she actually fallen in love with Nathan?

And if so, which one?

The one that had corresponded with her for a year on that internet chat room? Or the Nathan that had bedded her in San Pedro using *compromised* condoms? Was this to be my torment for coming up with such a duplicitous plan?

Weeks went by but the nagging questions and concerns still lingered in my mind. My conscious had never been pricked like this before, and with that came the realization that maybe it was because I had never truly loved a woman before, at least not the way that I loved Rian.

Ethan had contacted me the same day that I had received the phone call from Dr. Maxwell, letting me know that Rian was in fact, pregnant. I hadn't said a word to him about it. There was no need. I still was holding my breath; I needed to see what Rian was going to do with the knowledge that she was pregnant.

Ethan had told me that he had contacted Caroline. She had wanted to meet him, and they had met in Salt Lake City, where she now resides. As it turns out, Caroline long married now, has had no other children. She was delighted that Ethan had sought her out, and she received him very appreciatively. Maybe this had been a good move if nothing else, for that closure coming into place.

Two days have now gone by and I am waiting for Rian to come out of her room. We have dinner plans, and my stomach is in knots because I need to know how she is feeling about the pregnancy. I've been overly attentive to her since the holidays, which has been not only to assuage the guilt I've been feeling, but also seems to have made Rian happier and content, at least up until a couple of days ago.

"I'm ready, Preston," she says softly, coming out into the living room. "I'm sorry to have kept you waiting, but I'm just a bit tired today for some reason."

I look at her and my eyes penetrate hers, wishing like hell she felt comfortable enough to trust me with her *secret*. She's afraid of me, that can be the only reason.

But why?

I've never raised a hand to her. I've even spoke harshly to her that I can recall.

"Preston, what is it?" she asks, frowning.

I'm pulled from my thoughts by her voice. "You look different," I blurt. "Something is different about you, Rian, and I can't put my finger on it."

She is startled by my words. She shifts uncomfortably from one foot to the other, and I don't miss the fact she's biting her lower lip in apprehension. "I have a question that I've been putting off asking you, Preston. And maybe more than a question, I guess," her voice trailing off dejectedly.

"Let's start with the question," I reply, studying her carefully.

She looks up at me, hesitating just momentarily. "Did...you, I mean after your vasectomy---did you go back to your doctor and have yourself tested?"

I swallow. "Do you mean my sperm count?"

She nods.

"I did not," I lie, not taking my eyes from her. She visibly relaxes, and her eyes close for a moment. "Is there more?"

She nods again, and swallows nervously. "I'm afraid you might be angry with me," she starts, "I mean, I'm not sure how you're going to feel about this, but I can't keep it from you any longer. You see…"

I don't let her finish, because there's no way I'm going to let her confess her indiscretion to me. "Are you pregnant, darling?" I ask, making sure she can hear the happiness in my voice. "Because if you are, I want you to know how pleased that I am about it."

Her eyes lift to mine and she's searching for the truth.

She finds it.

"Yes, Preston, I am and I felt you…"

Again, I don't let her finish, because this moment is hers and it won't be spoiled. I pull her against me, stroking her hair gently, and nuzzling the top of her head. "You don't know how happy you've made me, Rian," I say softly to her.

"But what about Em?" she asks quietly.

"What about her?"

"Will she give you a divorce, Preston?"

Fuucckk…

Epilogue - Ethan's POV

I'm on the plane headed back East. Oh, not to Chicago where I live now. No, I'm heading to Boston. A last minute change of plans after meeting my real mother in Salt Lake City.

My real mother and I had a long talk. And I learned so much from her about my father---much more than I'd learned while growing up, that there was no way I could not face him again.

I'd told my mother, Caroline---I'd told her what my father had talked me into doing. I was ashamed to tell her, but it had prayed on my mind for months now, and she was the obvious one to hear it and not judge me for it. And she hadn't judged me at all. She'd recognized my anguish. She could emphasize with it as well.

"You're just getting a taste, Ethan, of what it is going to feel like having a child out there who doesn't even know you exist," she'd said, a single tear rolling down her cheek. "Don't let it happen if it's gonna eat you up. Maybe you're more me than you are him."

Her words played over and over again in my head as I looked out the window of the plane, seeing the thick, fluffy cloud layer that reminded me of the softness of Rian. That night had been so much more than simple fucking.

Her soft as velvet skin; her fingers digging deeply into my back as she came multiple times. Her mewling and moaning with each thrust of my cock inside of her tight pussy. Her creamy wetness at the touch of my tongue as I licked her essence over and over again.

Our connection had been much more than sexual. It had been an intimate coupling of two souls that were starving for a mating of not only our bodies, but our minds as well. And I didn't even know her mind until that night, but in those hours we spent together, as I pounded my flesh into her, taking supreme pleasure in knowing I was fucking her better than my old man ever could, I understood this beautiful woman.

And I had done my best to plant my seed inside of her, something my father confirmed in our last conversation I successfully achieved. Something he wasn't equipped to do, and yes, I took great satisfaction in that.

But here's the thing. The baby Rian is carrying is mine---not his. And the decent man inside won't allow me to walk away from this. At least not until Rian hears the whole story. Somebody owes her the truth. And that somebody is me. She will know how much the night we spent together meant to me---and how difficult it was for me to leave her there; to simply sneak away without a word or a promise---or an explanation.

The hell with my father and his money. I refuse to be just one more person my father's money can buy. I hope to fuck that Rian will forgive my part in the duplicity, and understand that I want to do the right thing where my child is concerned.

The End

About the Author

I hope you thoroughly enjoyed "The Other Man," and if you want to check out some of my other published titles or upcoming releases! They are just as naughty, with different characters, and new flavors of taboo---just for *you!*

How about some sneak peaks?

Dark Ride

Prudence Baker is home from college and working her part time job at the Rexall drug store in her sleepy little Southern hometown, which is still home to bigotry. Forget that it's 1977; her influential Daddy would never approve of her fascination with Nathan Crawl, a bold, black construction worker who's caught her eye and stirred up a craving inside of her that can only be appeased by him. Pru is treading in dangerous territory. And so is Nathan.

Adult Content 18+
Explicit Sexual Situations

Sneak Peek! (From "Dark Ride")

"Are you married, Nathan?" I asked succinctly.

"No, m'am."

"Good. I'm looking to see how black cock feels if you want to know the truth. You fascinated me from the first second I laid eyes on you. I hope---well, I hope I haven't offended you."

He took a moment before responding to me, and I held a breath, hoping like hell he wasn't going to tell me to get lost. But it was the truth I'd given him, no matter how weird or crazy it sounded, there was something that pulsed within me that wanted to see how it felt to have his big black cock filling the walls of my pussy.

I'd grown wet for him in those few brief seconds before he responded.

"Where?" he asked. "Where can we go so nobody sees this black dude fucking your pearly white pussy?"

Sherry Darling

While home from college over spring break, twenty-year-old Sherry Monroe is shocked to learn that her mother is having fertility issues, and even more shocked when she is approached by her stepfather with a plan on how to solve those issues.

Sometimes a kind heart can become a heart of stone when lust and betrayal enter the equation.

ADULT CONTENT/GRAPHIC SEXUAL SITUATIONS

Sneak Peek: Sherry Darling

His cock was in his hand; he was stroking it slowly and deliberately as he watched me.

It was huge.

I hadn't realized my stepfather was so well-endowed until this very moment. He sensed my fear and hesitation. "Don't be scared," he said softly when my eyes widened. "We'll make it work."

"Uh, I don't think it's going to fit, James."

"Lay back and relax," he replied softly. "It's all about foreplay and technique, trust me."

I did as I was told. His hands grasped my nightgown, pulling it off over my head. "There now," he said gazing down at me and sighing heavily. "God, you're so fucking beautiful."

His hand grasped my panties and lowered them down to my ankles and over my feet. I felt his calloused fingers gently caress my legs, moving up to my thighs, where he continued to lightly massage my skin. I shivered with delight and with anticipation, too. The fear was subsiding just as he said it would.

His fingers traveled to my pussy, and I could tell that I'd gotten moist with just the anticipation that tonight I was going to be fucked by a man.

And not just any man: my stepfather. The guy I had idolized for most of my life. The same guy who had taken care of me when I'd been sick as a child; had dropped me off at school each morning with a kiss on my cheek.

The same one who had grounded my ass when I'd missed curfew, and had insisted Jeremy come to the door whenever we went out on a date.

I felt his fingers ply at the sensitive folds of my pussy. "You're wet, baby. That's nice. Let's see if I can get you wetter. Your Mama loves it when I do what I'm about to do to you."

Making the Team

Ally and Jennifer are BFF's in college. Each of them are dating hot college football jocks, but when a game of swapping partners puts their friendship at stake, the girls find a way to work it out.

And their guys are right behind them!

Adult Content 18+
Explicit Sexual Situations

Sneak Peak! (From "Making the Team")

Ally and I were waiting in Mason's car, the heat jacked up on high, trying to get the blood flowing back into our extremities.

"So, how are you going to approach Mason?" I asked her from the back seat.

"Mason," she cooed, "will be a piece of cake. He's down with anything I want. I've already made the initial approach with him. He didn't seem surprised. He just gave me one of those looks, and said, 'We'll see, babe.' Besides that, I'm pretty sure he's been admiring that tight little perky ass of yours from afar for a while," she finished with a smirk. "You're gonna love his cock, trust me."

I felt my cheeks warm and my pussy clench at the thought of my best friend's dude having his cock buried balls deep inside my pussy, while she and Caden watched. I wasn't gonna lie, I could feel myself getting wet all over again.

"So, what are the rules? You watch us, and then we have to watch you guys without touching one another while we do? You know that's gonna be tough. You know how fucking horny I get watching online porn."

She giggled from the front seat, where she was turned to the side watching me. "That's why I want you and Mason to go first. I have no issue with self-control. My only concern will be making sure Caden doesn't go all alpha jealous when he sees Mason pumping his cock into your sweet, tight little pussy and hears you mewling my guy's name over and over again like a prayer."

In Conclusion

So, you've finished "The Other Man," and you've had some hot and steamy 'sneak peeks' at a few of my other novellas . . . are you MOIST?

LOL! Yeah, I know readers HATE that word, so let me correct that---ARE YOU DRIPPING WET?

Sorry, but in my honest opinion both of those words conjure up exactly what you're probably feeling, and it's not wrong. It's what these novellas are intended to do.

So, if you're wanting more, well then what is keeping you from 1-clicking the ebook, or ordering the paperback from Amazon? (I promise, it comes in a brown paper-wrapped package!)

Thanks for giving my steamy, sexy, and kind of taboo novellas a chance. I appreciate it, truly I do!

XOXO

Made in the USA
Columbia, SC
22 August 2017